Daydreams *for* Night

JOHN SOUTHWORTH

ILLUSTRATIONS BY

DAVID OUIMET

SIMPLY READ BOOKS

The Adventure *of* Big Lou *and* Little Louise

FOR MANY days and nights, Big Lou and Little Louise sailed the seas in a giant carved-out pumpkin. Together they battled endless rains, thunder, lightning, and enormous waves that threatened to topple and drown them as they made their brave way. When all had calmed the sun came out and shone its warm rays upon our two young adventurers. They soon became quite tired and were ready to fall into a long, yummy sleep. But just as they began to drift off, the sea turned a creamy white and began flowing through a growing hole that had burst in the bottom of the pumpkin.

"It's coconut milk!" cried Little Louise.

"Mmmm . . . my favorite," said Big Lou, licking it up.

Soon the giant pumpkin was full of coconut milk, and Big Lou and Little Louise had little choice but to abandon ship. After a while of swimming away from the sinking pumpkin, they climbed inside one of the tens of overgrown coconut rowboats, which had miraculously begun to pop up on the surface of the sea. And so, half-asleep and rather dumbfounded, Big Lou and Little Louise each rowed a little coconut rowboat back to shore, where they received a hero's welcome and were the envy of adventurers everywhere.

Fingus *the* Fisherman *and the* First Watermelon

MANY MOONS ago, Fingus the Fisherman discovered the world's first watermelon, lying on the grey pebbles of a small cove by the sea. "Such a strange-looking melon. It must have washed ashore," he thought. That night Fingus, his wife, and his three small girls agreed to eat the watermelon for supper. Everyone enjoyed it very much.

The next morning Fingus strolled down to the small cove, only to discover hundreds more watermelons covering each and every inch of the pebble beach. "My goodness," he muttered, "what 'ave we 'ere?" He took off his fisherman's cap and wiped his brow, feeling quite puzzled. But after a few minutes of gazing into the sad eyes of the sea, Fingus the Fisherman walked away from the watermelons and towards the dock. He spent the rest of the day fishing in his boat. Upon returning to shore, he saw a small army of chimney sweeps, lifting all the watermelons into wheelbarrows, and that evening, as chimney sweeps all across the land gobbled up their first watermelons for supper, Fingus the Fisherman walked home with a sack of haddock over his back, lost in thought.

Harry *the* Head Librarian

ONE DAY, Harry the Head Librarian was sitting at his desk in his office when a sunflower suddenly grew out of the top of his head. But he was too busy to notice. He spent that afternoon alone and immersed in his work, which required a great deal of concentration. Eventually, he got up to visit the water fountain. As he left his office, two young girls with golden braids, seeing the sunflower on top of Harry the Head Librarian's head, dropped a big pile of books. But again, Harry took no notice. As he waited behind three grade three boys who were covered in dirt and were drinking copious amounts of water at the fountain, Harry looked at his wristwatch and began to anxiously plan the rest of the day. The two young girls with golden braids approached him and said, "Mr. Harry, why do you have a sunflower on your head?"

Harry the Head Librarian replied, "Check the Gardening Section, bottom shelf, row nine."

Girl Guide Cookies

FOR TWO years running, Ester had sold more Girl Guide cookies than any other Brownie in the whole province. Every day after school, Ester would go knocking on as many people's doors or walking into as many stores as possible, trying her very best to sell as many boxes of cookies as she could. Which she did! One day Ester decided to knock on the door of the Ralph J. Henning Funeral Home. As the door opened, Ester, in her best and brightest ten-year-old voice said, "Good day, Sir. Would you care to buy some Girl Guide cookies? All proceeds to charity!" But the tall thin man that stood before her did not answer. He was pale white and odd-looking, and his dark suit seemed very odd too. He stared at Ester for a while, and then, with a very slow and deliberate gesture, shook his head and closed the door.

A month later, Ester quit the Girl Guides altogether and withdrew to her bedroom, where she stayed for three whole years, drawing strange-looking circles and grotesque portraits of her parents.

The Secret Lawn Bowling Society

WHEN SUMMER is in full swing, and the nights are especially hot and sticky, something quite secret and quite wonderful takes place on a soft green lawn at the end of an old oak park. A dozen slightly tipsy old ladies, giggling and wiggling and whispering like schoolgirls, will secretly gather to lawn bowl in the yellow moonlight, wearing absolutely nothing at all. When the first signs of dawn appear, the bare old ladies of the secret lawn bowling society tiptoe across the park and swim across a warm pond filled with sleeping swans. Upon reaching the other side, they are greeted by a flock of well-dressed old gents in bowler hats, patiently holding pink-dotted white towels in the morning mist.

Railroad *to the* Moon

OVER THE last summer, hundreds of sleepwalking conductors and pale porters have taken to building the world's first railroad to the moon. Soon folks from all over will be able to visit the moon on board a luxurious train made out of old streetcars and cobblestones. Last month tickets went on sale for the first trip, but so far only Silly Cindy and her dancing bear have bought one.

The Strange Man Who Kept *a* Ferris Wheel *in* His Back Yard

THERE ARE hundreds of little homes that sit very close to one another along the little river that runs through the town. It seems that everybody wants to live by the river. One man in particular moved all the way from out west. His name was Earl. He was a small, quiet man with big ears and a white mustache, who always wore the same rather tattered suit and tie. One day, a big truck carrying three giant moving men and a huge Ferris wheel appeared outside Earl's door. Slowly, a small crowd gathered to see what was all the fuss. It was soon agreed that it would be best to unload the Ferris wheel in Earl's back garden, which meant driving around back, lifting it across the river, and somehow fitting it in the small confines of Earl's yard, which they did. Earl gave them a small tip and a cup of hot cider and the three men drove away.

Later that year, Earl managed to get the Ferris wheel operating, and everyone in the neighborhood became excited for a while and lined up for a ride before they went to school or on the way home from work. When the winter came Earl shut down the Ferris wheel for good. On some snowy nights when all was quiet, Earl would bring out a flask of hot cider to a pale young man dressed in second-hand funeral clothes that he'd find curled up on one of the Ferris wheel seats.

The Boy Who Was Made *of* Wood

THE BOY who was made of wood was deathly afraid of the rain and even more afraid of the sun. So much so that at the age of four he ran away to live beneath an old, forgotten railroad bridge. One day, after many cold and lonely weeks, he decided he'd had enough. Shivering and ashen, he slowly crept from underneath the bridge and onto a small slope of tall grass. When the sun finally came out the boy who was made of wood was so tired and beat, he promptly feel asleep. For two whole days he slept through the warm sun and a little rain too. When he woke he was covered head to toe in bright green leaves.

Little Girls

ONCE A year, at the end of April, hundreds or more little girls in bright red petticoats and blue-buckle shoes hop along unused railroad tracks holding hands and singing the fairy national anthem:

"Fairy oh fairy be merry be hairy,
But please don't be shy,
We won't be much longer,
Coo-coo! Coo-coo!"

After a day and a half or so of traveling, the little girls find themselves a giant oak tree to nap beneath. There is not much more to this story, only to say that when they awake, they miraculously find themselves back home nestled in their warm beds with sparkling candy-covered acorns all over their heads!

The Boy *with* Grey Hair

THE EIGHT-YEAR-OLD boy whose hair had turned completely grey did not enjoy going to school, as he was constantly being ridiculed. Instead, he liked to spend his days on a big Latvian cargo ship, which had recently docked in the harbor and was being loaded with sacks of fresh potatoes. One day, his mother and father, who were both sick with worry, were horrified to find their little grey-haired boy at a table with three Latvian sailors in the ship's kitchen, singing sad sea shanties and peeling potatoes.

Night *in the* Aquarium

WHEN THE sun has set, and every trainer, tour guide, cafeteria cook, janitor, and paying customer has long gone home, the aquarium becomes a very quiet place. The only person left behind is Kimron the night security guard, a tall middle-aged man from Grenada, with bright brown eyes and a big wide smile. In the early morning hours, Kimron makes long, high-pitched sounds, in a strange and haunting falsetto, as he ambles around the giant water tanks filled with dolphins, beluga whales, and deep sea fishes. In the morning, Kimron takes a bus back to his wife and two teenage sons on the edge of the city, his belly filled with a soft tingling.

The Whale Who Lived
on a Faraway Hill

THE WHALE who lived on a faraway hill was feeling very blue, mostly because she was still unsure as to how she ever managed to be living on a faraway hill in the first place and also because she missed the sea very much. After many weeks of spouting nothing but hot air and drowning in her misery, she began to slowly make her way down. When she finally reached the bottom of the hill, she found herself in a small mining town. The kind-hearted people of the small mining town had never seen such a worried-looking whale before.

So they went immediately to work, filling their biggest mining pit with lake water. Then, with the help of thirty of their strongest miners, they lifted the whale and lowered her into their new man-made lake. The whale was happy and she started to cry. With all the townspeople looking on from the side, the whale sang the most beautiful song they had ever heard. It was so beautiful that all the whales in all the oceans heard it, and they too sang out with joy, and the whale who had lived on a faraway hill trembled with love.

The Magic Box *with the* Elephant

THE MAGIC box with the elephant painted on its side is the prize possession of Glen Daly, a retired bricklayer, who lives in an old folks' home that faces the sea. Glen first heard the swirling circus music that churned and turned in the magic box while sitting on the floor of his grandfather's cluttered workroom as a boy.

Tonight, when everyone is asleep, Glen will dress in his best navy blue suit and take the magic box with the elephant painted on its side all the way down the winding steps to the stony beach, where he will sit and listen once more, as if it was the first night of his life.

For Janine—J.S.
For Michamar—D.O.

Published in 2014 by Simply Read Books
www.simplyreadbooks.com

Text © 2014 John Southworth
Illustrations © 2014 David Ouimet

Library and Archives Canada Cataloguing in Publication
Southworth, John, author
Daydreams for night /written by John Southworth ;
illustrated by David Ouimet.
Short stories.
ISBN 978-1-927018-17-0 (bound)

I. Ouimet, David, illustrator II. Title.

PS8637.O96D39 2014   C813'.6   C2013-906098-7

We gratefully acknowledge for their financial support of our
publishing program the Canada Council for the Arts, the BC Arts Council,
and the Government of Canada through the Canada Book Fund (CBF).

Manufactured in Malaysia
Book design by Naomi MacDougall

10 9 8 7 6 5 4 3 2 1